Harry, Mari and Squib
and the Mystery of Miss Tree

Marigold Masters, Mari for short, likes to solve mysteries. So does Harry Hardcastle, Harry-the-Hawk Hardcastle for long, and together they form the We-Solve-It Detective Agency. Harry's young brother Squib tags along as well, but there's safety in numbers and he's useful too. In this first story the trio solve the mystery of Miss Tree, Prickly Pear City's favourite dance teacher. Has she been kidnapped? Why else would she cancel dancing lessons at short notice? And why do the neighbours want to try to stop Miss Tree putting on a performance of *Peter Pan*?

Harry, Mari and Squib set out to unravel the mystery – and what a time they have!

The first case for Harry, Mari and Squib. Look out for more!

Jana Hunter lived in America for many years, where private detective agencies abound. She now lives in Leicester with her husband and son, where she is a full-time writer of children's books.

Jana Hunter

Harry, Mari and Squib and the Mystery of Miss Tree

Illustrated by Noel Ford

PUFFIN BOOKS

PUFFIN BOOKS

Published by the Penguin Group
Penguin Books Ltd, 27 Wrights Lane, London w8 5tz, England
Penguin Books USA Inc., 375 Hudson Street, New York, New York 10014, USA
Penguin Books Australia Ltd, Ringwood, Victoria, Australia
Penguin Books Canada Ltd, 10 Alcorn Avenue, Toronto, Ontario, Canada m4v 3b2
Penguin Books (NZ) Ltd, 182–190 Wairau Road, Auckland 10, New Zealand

Penguin Books Ltd, Registered Offices: Harmondsworth, Middlesex, England

First published 1993
1 3 5 7 9 10 8 6 4 2

Text copyright © Jana Novotny Hunter, 1993
Illustrations copyright © Noel Ford, 1993
All rights reserved

The moral right of the author has been asserted

Typeset by DatIX International Limited, Bungay, Suffolk
Filmset in Monophoto Garamond
Printed in England by Clays Ltd, St Ives plc

Chapter One

Saturday 19 June, 8 a.m.

Another day in Prickly Pear City.

I am up at my window, taking notes.

Prickly Pear Street bakes in the early sun. . . two floors down, empty and hot.

I write it down . . . *someone's* got to do it.

I'm a Detective.

A Private Eye, name of Marigold Masters. Marigold was Mum's idea. She got it when she first saw my orange sticky-out hair. (I only just escaped being called Carrot.) Nowadays friends call me Mari. Rhymes with Harry.

Harry's my partner: Harry-the-Hawk Hardcastle. We're the We-Solve-it Detective Agency.

The We-Solve-It Agency is on the top floor of a block of flats. It's where I live.

From up here I can witness any crime. Yes, any. OK, up till yesterday maybe the only crime I witnessed was a kid licking his baby brother's lollipop.

But all that changed last night. It started off like any other Friday night. I was in bed with *The Dead Rat's Paw* and a cup of cocoa . . .

It was late.

Suddenly I heard a noise. Not the usual cat-squalling, car-door-slamming kind of noise, but something so spine-chilling I almost choked on my cocoa.

"Squawk! Squawk! Squaaaaawk!"

Now if this was a jungle in wildest Africa, a squawk like that would be a normal thing to hear. But not here. Not on Prickly Pear Street.

So, faster than a jet-propelled frog, I leapt up to my window.

Outside, parked in front of Pear Tree School of Dance and Drama, was a van. A suspicious-looking van.

Obviously it was part of a fiendish plot because the squawk was coming from inside. Then a voice spoke:

"Aaagh! Help! Aaagh! Help!"

Suffering squirrels! A speaking squawk!

Maybe I should've climbed back into bed and minded my own business. Maybe. But then I would never have solved the strangest mystery ever to hit Prickly Pear.

And, let's face it, mysteries are my business.

So, grabbing my jacket, I slipped out of the flat and ran downstairs. Barefoot.

(On my way, I made a discovery. Bare feet are fine for creeping past your mum, but *agony* when running across gravel.)

Outside, Prickly Pear Street was deserted. Silent. Even the lamps cast a sleepy glow. But inside Pear Tree School it was all action! Noise – crashing, banging, electric-drilling.

Weird.

Now I admit that Miss Tree, who owns Pear Tree School of Dance and Drama, is a pretty unusual lady. She's given to dancing on her toes and singing Scottish Highland ballads late at night. But crashing and banging about? Never. She is as light as a feather on her feet.

So what was Pear Tree's favourite dance teacher up to tonight? It was what you might call a Miss Tree mystery.

Crouched behind her bushes for almost an hour, I began to wonder whether she was with a gang of bank robbers, now tunnelling their way to the Prickly Pear City Bank. Or perhaps a crazed scientist had bred giant woodpeckers who were at this very moment burrowing through the school walls.

Finally I decided the house was cursed. Poltergeists were tapping out messages . . . sending furniture flying.

Furniture . . . beds. That made me think of my own bed. It was a lovely bed. Warm, snuggly . . . Only a fool would leave a bed like that.

A fool or a detective.

Suddenly, the door to Miss Tree's

opened. I ducked down low as a massive boot crunched centimetres away from my nose.

"That should hold if you're daft enough to try flying," said an odd singsong voice, with a laugh. "I've done a really thorough job this time."

Hold her? Thorough job?

Blistering Birdseed! Had the man tied up Miss Tree? Was that *her* squawk for help?

This was serious. Too serious for one person, even if I was a detective.

So I waited for the van to drive off and ran back home.

First thing the next morning, I call Harry.

"Harry?"

"Mari! What has an orange head, is long and skinny and goes at a speed of ninety miles an hour?"

Another of Harry's jokes. He's always making them up about me. "OK, Harry, What *is* long and skinny and goes at ninety miles an hour?"

Harry gives a snort of laughter. 'A Belisha beacon with an outboard motor!"

Ignoring his crazed laughter, I say, "Harry, listen. Something strange is going on."

"No kidding,' says Harry. "Anything to do with Miss Tree?"

Harry is smart, but this was

positively psychic!

"Good gravy, Harry. How did you know?"

"She just cancelled my class."

Of course! My class is Monday, but Harry usually spends Saturdays polishing floor-boards with his feet, along with other dancers in Prickly Pear. He's good too.

"Harry?"

"Yes?"

"You'd better get over here right away. I think we're on to something big."

"Big? Wow."

"That's right, Harry . . . *Wow*. Miss Tree is in trouble. She needs our help."

"Help?"

"Is there an echo on this line? Yes, help, Harry."

"Why?"

"Because, Harry, *I think Miss Tree's been kidnapped*."

Chapter Two

While I'm waiting for Harry, I keep
Pear Tree School under surveillance.
(Keeping Under Surveillance means
watching a suspicious area.)

Suddenly the door next to the school
opens. Out steps Mrs Brown with her
puppy, Loopy. 7.45 a.m. on the dot.

I make the usual notes:

Yeuk! Fouling the footpath is a crime punishable by a £20 fine. That's the second time this week Mrs Brown's let it happen. Something must be done.

But until Miss Tree has been rescued, crimes like Fouling the Footpath will have to wait, I decide.

Anyway, the doorbell is ringing so I go to answer it.

"Sorry about Squib," says Harry. "Mum made me bring him."

Squib is Harry's little brother. He is OK as far as kid brothers go, but he doesn't do much for our image as Professional Detectives.

"Just stay cool, kid," I say.

"OK." Squib's eyes shine like chocolate buttons floating in milk. He doesn't usually investigate cases.

Come to think of it, neither do we. This is our first "biggy".

Over juice and biscuits, I brief Harry.

(Briefing is telling someone working on the case what's been happening.)

"Kidnapping's a dirty business, Harry," I warn.

"Right," Harry says. "No time to wash."

"Can you be serious for a minute?"

"OK."

"Now," I flip open my notebook, "what do you know about this puzzling case?"

Harry gets his "Detective" look. "Well," he says, "Miss Tree phoned this morning. She told Mum she was a bit tied up, but classes would be back to normal on Monday."

"Tied up?" I write it down. "How did she sound?"

"My mum? Fine."

"Not your mum, Harry. Miss Tree."

"Oh." Harry grins. "She sounded fine too."

"Maybe she had a gun pointed at her head. Seems to me she was hinting about being tied up."

"Wow! We just thought she was busy."

"I knew she was tied up," Squib says.

I smile at Squib. "Who'd believe Miss Tree's been kidnapped? Crimes like that don't happen in Prickly Pear City. We need to find her." I pace the floor. (Detectives do that to help them think.) "Until we find her, no one is going to believe us. We're in this thing alone, Harry."

"Me too!" shouts Squib.

"You're supposed to stay quiet," Harry says. "Watch the experts at work."

"Right. What do we have?" I read out from my notebook: "Suspect wears boots. Victim taken in van." I pace the floor faster. "I can almost hear the kidnapper . . . creeping behind her . . . stalking . . . *lurking* . . ."

"Harry, when I say, 'let's put our heads together,' this is *not* what I mean." I rub my head. "OK, let's get on. What else do we know about the victim?"

Harry clears his throat. "Well, she's worried."

"Worried?"

"Yes."

"Go on, Harry."

"There've been complaints. The neighbours say Pear Tree School is too noisy."

"How bad can a few kids dancing be?"

Harry shrugs. "Mr Parker says it's like living next door to a herd of fairy elephants in Doc Martens."

"Very funny."

"That's not all. Mr Brown says that when we do tap-dancing his whole house shakes. Last week when he was squirting ketchup on his dinner, the table shook so much he ended up with a plateful of sausage and chips in his lap and ketchup up his nose."

"What a sauce! Was he having his

own Red Nose Day, or what?"

Harry laughs. "Seriously, though, the neighbours are trying to stop Miss Tree from putting on *Peter Pan*."

"But the whole of Prickly Pear is coming to see *Peter Pan*!" I say. "It's going to be such fun."

Peter Pan is our end-of-term production this year. Miss Tree adapted it herself. It's like the original, except everyone (even the crocodile) dances.

"You know Miss Tree's neighbours hate crowds or fun," says Harry. "They'll do all they can to stop it. Brown says people will pinch his parking spot. He loves that stupid parking spot. He probably kisses it every night before he goes to bed."

"But, Harry, Miss Tree needs the money from ticket sales," I point out. "The class fees are so low, the only way she keeps the school open is by putting on shows."

"Right. If *Peter Pan* doesn't go on, Miss Tree says she'll have to close down," says Harry. "For good."

THE PRICKLY PEAR POST

PETER PAN WILL NEVER FLY TO NEVER NEVER LAND

COMPLAINING NEIGHBOURS GET THEIR WAY

"Harry, are you thinking what I'm thinking?"

"I think so. What are you thinking?"

"I'm thinking the kidnapper is someone who wants the school closed. Someone who'll hold Miss Tree hostage until there's no time left to do the show."

"That's just what I was thinking!"

"If we find the kidnapper, we can find Miss Tree. We need a drawing of the suspect. All we have is a boot. Think you can do it, Harry?" (Harry's an ace artist. He did all our Identikit drawings. Noses, mouths, chins, eyes, but no boots.)

"Sure, I can do it, partner. Just call me Quickdraw." Harry points his pencils like cowboy guns. "Pow! Pow!"

"Stick to pencil lead, Harry," I say. "Remember we at the We-Solve-It Agency are into non-violence."

"Yeah, guns hurt," Squib says. "We don't like to hurt people, do we, Mari?"

"Oh, right, I forgot."

Harry draws.

"That's it! Harry, you're brilliant."

"You noticed." Harry huffs on his finger-nails. "Are you a detective, by any chance?"

I look at the drawing of the boot. "I wonder what this booted kidnapper did to make Miss Tree squawk like that."

"Force-fed her with crackers?" suggests Harry.

"I know!" says Squib. "They locked her in a cage!"

"H'm, gagged her, more like. I think the kidnapper just wants her out of the way for a bit. He's probably taken her somewhere and locked her up. But where? Are you listening to me, Harry? Harry?"

"Mari, look over at the school," says Harry. "There's something going on."

Across the road we see a group of kids gathering around Miss Tree's front door.

"Uh-oh, trouble. It's time we got over there." I turn up the collar of my shirt. "Stay cool, partner."

Harry backs away. "Er, I think my mum needs help with the shopping."

"Harry. Miss Tree is in trouble." I grab Harry and pull up his collar. "We *have* to find her, Harry."

"OK, OK. No need to get physical."

Squib pulls his hat down low. "Let's go, Mari."

"Let's go."

We go.

Chapter Three

Outside the school a bunch of kids gathers. They are led by Mai Ling, Stretch and Pete. Miss Tree's nine o'clock class.

"Hiya," says Harry casually. "What's happening?"

Stretch (Tony Stretter) points to a note pinned to Miss Tree's front door. "Look!"

"It's strange," says Mai Ling. "Miss Tree never cancels."

"Harry, d'you recognize the writing?" I whisper.

Harry frowns. "Mari, it's *signed* 'Miss Tree'."

"I know, Harry. Detectives always check facts."

"Oh, yes." He studies the writing. "It's Tree's all right."

I make a note of this. Miss Tree's writing is dead scribbly. Maybe the kidnapper forced her to write it. Either that or her writing always looks like homework done on the top of the 59 bus.

"Where *is* Miss Tree?" says Pete. "She's not answering the door."

Squib draws a mega-breath. "It's a *secret*! We're on a case."

"*Squib!*" I shout. "Er, it's not a secret," I go on quickly. "Just Squib being funny."

"You'd better tell us, Mari." Stretch pulls himself up to his full one-metre height. "It's our teacher who's missing."

"Um, well. Miss Tree isn't missing exactly. It's just that she can't . . . she can't teach." (Whew!)

"Can't teach?"

"That's right. She can't teach today . . . er, on account . . . on account of her verruca."

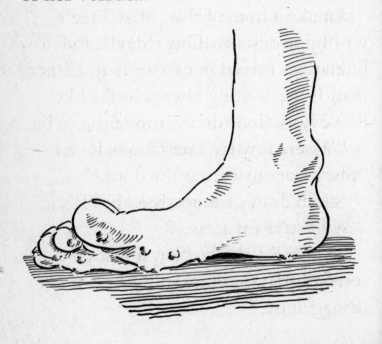

"*Verruca!*"

Verrucae impress these kids. Many's the time they've had to miss swimming because of their verrucae.

"Yes, verruca," I say quickly. "They're very catching. The doctor said Miss Tree had to cancel classes or the whole school would be infected."

Mai Ling looks sad. "Miss Tree said she might have to close the school. Is it because of her feet?"

"I don't know. One thing I do know is the school won't close down if Harry and I can help it."

"My sister Sadie hopes the school *will* close down," Stretch blurts out unexpectedly.

"Oh?" I try not to look surprised. "Why's that?"

"So she can take hang-gliding lessons on Saturdays. All she thinks of is flying."

It was true. Even now the sounds of Sadie being a jet plane were coming from the Stretters' upstairs window.

I like Sadie Stretter. She's the kind of girl who loves to feel the wind in her hair and twenty miles of air beneath her. I hoped she wasn't mixed up in this.

But she wanted the school closed down. And that gave her a motive.

Sighing, I add her to the list of suspects. If Sadie *was* the kidnapper she'd be charged. But at least she's innocent until proven guilty.

Pete takes a piece of chalk from his pocket. "How about a game of hopscotch, gang? Want to play, Squib?"

I nod at Squib. "Go ahead. Just keep cool, OK?"

"OK. *I won't say a word,*" whispers Squib, giving me an enormous wink.

Squib's sweet, but he's about as cool as Curried Chicken with Ginger-nuts.

We leave him arguing with the kids about who goes first. They're so busy, they ignore my request to clean up the mess lying near the number two.

Sighing, I rip out a page from my notebook and scoop it up.

Fighting crime. Keeping the streets clean.

Someone's got to do it.

And someone's got to find Miss Tree.

"Let's go, Harry," I say.

Chapter Four

It's time to talk to witnesses.

"You're the only one who witnessed anything," Harry says. "Want me to interview you?"

"Harry, we don't know that. Anyway, talking to witnesses is police procedure."

"Oh, right." Harry knocks on the Browns' door.

"You know Harry, there's another mystery I'd like to solve one day."

"What's that?"

"Why people who hate kids live near schools."

Harry shrugs. "One of the secrets of the Universe. Maybe the answer's floating somewhere in a time-warp."

"*Yes?*" interrupts an irritable voice.

"What is it?" Mrs Brown is standing in her doorway.

"Ahem, Detectives Masters and Hardcastle, ma'am."

We show our badges.

Mr Brown's voice floats down from upstairs. "Is it those kids again? Tell them they can't have their ball back."

Brown keeps all our balls. He must have a zillion by now. Ball Heaven.

"Mr Brown, sir, we'd just like to ask you a few questions about next door," I call out.

"Next door! I'll tell you about next door!" Brown shouts dramatically. "Bad enough with the dancing! Now it's banging! Drilling! Noise, noise, noise!" He's working himself into a lather big enough to do the laundry. "It's got to stop!"

Mrs Brown looks flustered. "We didn't get much sleep last night. That school will have to close down . . . So many children. Shouldn't be allowed in a residential street. I must go. My husband doesn't like to be disturbed on Saturdays."

Or any day.

"Ma'am, can you just tell us if you saw a van last night?" asks Harry.

But she has already closed the door.

I bend down and shout through the keyhole, "Mrs Brown, did you see anyone wearing boots enter the school?"

"Er, yes. I think so."

"Can you describe him?"

"He was small . . . curly hair." Mrs Brown's voice is fading as she walks up the stairs. "His name's Barney . . ."

"Anything else?" I shout.

But there's no reply. She's gone in to Mr Brown. From a bedroom window we hear her trying to calm the big bear down. "Now, dear, they were only here a minute . . ."

You'd think our visit was timed.

"Great, Harry!" I hug him. "We now have a name and a description."

Harry smiles. "We-Solve-It is on the trail."

"Come on. Let's see if Nosey Parker knows anything."

Mr Parker opens the door before we even get up the pathway. He spends most of his time at the window. If ever

I need another detective, Nosey Parker would be perfect. But I'm not sure I could stand his humour. His jokes are more corny than a tin of Niblets.

"Having a break from break dancing, kids?" He laughs.

"Classes have been cancelled for a bit," Harry explains.

I show my badge before Parker cracks any more howlers. "Detective Marigold Masters, sir. We-Solve-It Detective Agency. Like to ask a few questions about next door."

"You mean Twinkletoe Academy?" Nosey Parker does a little tap-dance. "Place is closing down."

"That's only a rumour," I say. "Just give us the facts, please, sir."

"If it's not closing down, why were the removers here?" he says. "Seen 'em myself last night."

Removers? Perhaps that banging last night *was* furniture being shifted. Only not by ghosts.

"Can you describe the van, Mr Parker?"

"Ordinary van. Blue. 'Maskerade' written on the side." He kills himself laughing. "They should learn to spell!"

"Maskerade." I write it in my notebook. "Thank you, Mr Parker. You've been most helpful."

Chapter Five

"Harry." I look at my watch. "Time's running out. We'd better follow the Maskerade lead."

"You go," Harry says. "I'll get a statement from Sadie."

(Statements are writing down everything a suspect says and having them sign on the bottom. (The bottom of the statement, that is.))

I nod. "Details, Harry. Remember them. Find out what everyone was doing Friday night. *In detail.*"

Harry salutes. "I'll be able to tell you the colour of their boxer shorts by the time I'm finished."

I find the address for Maskerade in the phone directory. It isn't far away — if you like walking.

Squib doesn't.
I keep him going with banana chips.

When we arrive, the shop is still open.

Nothing about removals.
Inside, I gasp. My mum should see
this. She said if there were awards for
messy rooms mine would win every
time. But this shop was a definite

contender. It was like something Aladdin uncovered, though he'd have had trouble finding the lamp.

Piles of costumes, masks and make-up cover the counter and hang from every wall. Bits of scenery are propped against stacks of paint-pots and ladders, while spotlights lean drunkenly together.

It's another world.

I stare at a huge painted dragon's head, while Squib is transfixed by the executioner's costume hanging from the dungeon wall.

For a moment nothing happens. Then, suddenly . . . *something moves*.

It is a hideous one-eyed monster . . . with a nose like a fist. A nose covered with festering boils.

I jump back like something on video rewind.

"Aaagh!"

If you ask me, *he* needs the help. A few buckets of Clearasil for a start.

"Er, I'm looking for the owner."

"That's me me me me," sings a voice from behind the mask.

And that's when I realize. *It's the kidnapper's voice!* I am face-to-mask with the kidnapper!

My detective manual says you must keep eye contact with suspects. But how can I do that with a papier-mâché eye dripping down the suspect's face?

"Er . . . I . . . I was wondering if you knew a Miss Tree. Runs Pear Tree School of Dance and Drama?"

"Miss Tra-la-la-la Treeeee?" Mask Face sings.

"Yes." I show my badge. "Detective Marigold Masters. We-Solve-It Detective Agency. We have reason to believe your shop made a delivery to the school last night."

"Me . . . me . . . meeeee?" sings old Mask Face.

"Yes."

Suddenly there's a cracking sound as Squib tightens his hold on my hand. "OW!"

"Mariiiii . . .?" he whimpers.

"OK, Squib," I whisper. "We're going in just a minute." I look the Masked Man right in the eye. "Could you just tell us, sir? What did you deliver . . . or *pick up*?"

The Masked Man begins to sing. Softly, then louder. It's bad enough when a suspect sings, but when the song comes from behind a hideous mask . . . it's positively eerie. What's more, I've heard better singing in a Friday Morning Infant Assembly.

He's still giving his solo as we turn and run. Fast.

Song of the Masked Man

There was a dance teacher named Tree
Wanting Peter Pan *stuff hurriedly.*
She got costumes for the stage,
A parrot in a cage,
And flying equipment from me!

Chapter Six

The Masked Man calls after us but we keep right on running.

We're not stupid. *Brave*, but not stupid.

"That eye . . ." Squib says. "He had only *one eye* . . ."

"Who'd want two like that?"

Squib pants.

At least, I *think* Squib pants. I have never known him pant that loud before. It sounds more like a mastiff than a boy. A wolfhound.

The Hound of the Baskervilles!

"Squib?" I say.

"Y-yes?"

"I think we're being followed. Run faster, Squib!"

But the faster we run, the louder the

panting gets. Then a voice adds to the yelping and panting.

"Crusher! Stop, Crusher!"

Crusher?

Who'd be a detective? Run. Run. Run. Round corners. Down alleys. Up

streets. Run, run, run. On and on
until . . .

"I'm sorry," says the dog's owner. "Crusher thought you were just having fun."

"*Fun?* I've had more fun doing a Monday Morning Maths Test!" I rub my bottom.

The girl laughs and shakes her purple (yes, purple) head. "He thought it was a game. If anyone runs, Crusher chases. Look, my name's Pansy Potts. That's my shop over there. Pansy's Pet Parlour. Come over and I'll see what I can do about that knee."

I look at Crusher. I look at my bleeding knee. What have I got to lose? Only a leg.

"Squib, wait outside. Get help if I'm not out in five minutes."

It's the usual kind of pet shop. Smells, noises and animals. There is also every kind of equipment necessary to pet lovers, including Pooper Scoopers.

Squib gets a big welcome from the

gerbils in the window. He's desperate for a pet, but his mum's allergic.

Smiling, Pansy sits me down. "Cute little fellas, gerbils." She wipes my knee with something that stings like ten angry wasps having a bad day.

"Ouch!"

"It'll stop hurting soon."

"Yesterday's not soon enough for me."

Pansy laughs. "I like you. You're funny. By the way," she says, "why were you running? Are you in training for something?"

"OW! Not exactly. Oh . . . Ooohhh." Suddenly I remember who's supposed to ask the questions. "We're on a case." I show my badge. "We-Solve-It Detective Agency."

"Great badge," Pansy says admiringly.

"Made it myself." I clear my throat. "Anyway, er, ever seen anything like this?" I show the drawing of the kidnapper's boot.

Pansy Potts stares at it. She adjusts her pink-tinted glasses. "H'm. A twelve-eyed, long-headed monster with an enormous tongue . . ."

I turn the card the right way up. "It's a boot."

Pansy giggles. "Oops. Well now, let me see. What's this boot done? Muddied floors? Kicked someone?"

"Maybe." I guess I could trust her. "Actually, it belongs to a kidnapper. Kidnapped our teacher."

"Kidnapped?"

I nod.

"Your teacher?"

"Dance teacher. Miss Tree. Wears a red cape."

"A red cape?" Pansy thinks for a minute. "Wait a minute. Someone wearing a red cape bought a parrot yesterday!"

"A parrot?"

"Norwegian Blue."

"H'm. I wonder." I put the drawing back in my pocket. Things are starting to fall into place. "OK . . . OK, thanks for the help, Pansy."

"Any time."

We say goodbye to Pansy, Crusher and the gerbils and start walking. It is 12.03 p.m.

Lunch-time.

Suddenly it hits me.

"Wait here," I tell Squib. "I just thought of something."

Fighting crime. Keeping the streets clean.

It's my job.

Chapter Seven

Back in the We-Solve-It office, Harry gives his report. "Sadie's in the clear."

"I knew Sadie was no kidnapper. She *never* wears boots."

"She has a cast-iron alibi."

(Alibis prove you were doing something else when the crime was committed.)

"Let's hear it, Harry."

Harry clears his throat and reads from his notebook. "On the night in question, Sadie Stretter was practising parachute jumps from her top-bunk bed."

"Witnesses?"

"Mother. Says the whole house shook."

I nod. "Any other suspects?"

Harry flips over the page to a list of names and answers. "Nope. Everybody on Prickly Pear Street seems to have been busy when the kidnapping took place."

"Well, I think we've found the kidnapper. I'm pretty sure it's Barney. But I can't give a description. He was wearing a mask." I show Harry the words to Barney's song. "What d'you make of it, Harry?"

Harry reads. "Sounds like Miss Tree got things from Barney for *Peter Pan*."

"Exactly. So why would he kidnap a client?"

"Unpaid bills?" offers Harry.

"Nooo . . . It doesn't make sense. Harry, what's that rumbling noise?"

"My stomach. I'm starving."

"Me too."

"Me three!" says Squib.

"Let's eat."

Lunch is spaghetti hoops on buttered toast. Harry toasts and I butter. Squib spills milk.

"The mask was dead creepy," I say, soaking up spaghetti sauce with my last bit of toast. "Like something out of a horror film."

"I wasn't scared," lies Squib.

"Detectives must be tough," says Harry grandly. "It's our job."

"Right," I say. "Oh, and, Harry?"

"Yes?"

"They must be clean too. Wipe the spaghetti sauce off your chin."

We all crack up laughing. But suddenly we freeze as the room is lit by a strange flash of light. It flickers across the kitchen and bounces off the pots.

"What's that?"

There's another flash. Then another. Two shorts, one long.

A signal!

And that's not all. They're coming from Miss Tree's downstairs window.

And parked outside her school is the Maskerade van.

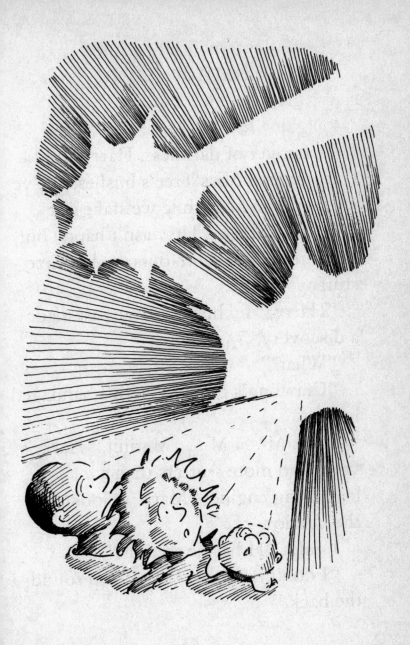

Chapter Eight

Under cover of darkness, Harry and I creep behind Miss Tree's bushes. We've left Squib in bed while we stake out Pear Tree School. He wasn't happy but, as we told him, stake-outs are big time stuff.

"Harry," I whisper. "I've just made a discovery."

"What?"

"Crawling's not easy with a bandaged leg."

"Ssh. M . . . M . . . Mariiiii." Harry's voice had more stutters than a backfiring engine. "Mari . . . look! In the window . . ."

I gulp. "H-has he seen us?"

"I don't think so. Let's creep round the back."

My legs go wobbly, suddenly. The ground beneath them feels like a Bouncy Castle.

"I'm scared," I whisper. "This might be dangerous."

Harry nods. "Mummy!" he mouths silently.

Quickly, silently we make a dash for the wall and slide along it. We really look like detectives now.

Pear Tree School is a tall brick house with big French windows. Miss Tree keeps the windows open in summer while we practise. (It can get pretty sweaty in the studio.) Tonight the windows are open as usual but across them are drawn heavy curtains. We can't see a thing.

We can't see, but we can hear. First we hear a *clank whirr, clank whirr*, like a pulley lifting a heavy load, then Miss Tree's voice: "I can fly! I can fly! I can fly . . . Wheeeee!"

Poor Miss Tree! Had she lost her mind and found a parrot's instead? What had Barney done to her? Fed her on nothing but breadcrumbs and water?

"Harry," I whisper. "Let me climb on your shoulders. I want to see over the curtains."

Harry groans. "I just remembered I have to be in bed by ten."

"Harry, this is no time for jokes. Bend down."

Harry bends and I climb.

"Harry?" I whisper grabbing on to the door-frame. "What's that panting noise?"

"Probably me. You're very heavy."

"It's so loud. I've heard it before . . . It reminds me of . . . Harryyyyy!"

"Hello!" Miss Tree waves to us from above as she swoops across the stage.

"I didn't expect to see you two."

"M-Miss Tree," I say, weakly looking at the invisible wire holding her up. "You were here all the time . . ."

Harry groans. "Where am I? Is this a nightmare?"

Everything around us seems to be flying. Dog fur, feathers, Crusher. He barks and bounds about as the parrot dives and screeches like something let off on Bonfire Night.

For a while we're stunned. Dizzy.

Then Miss Tree breaks in with a laugh. "What an entrance! It would be great for *Peter Pan*!"

Suddenly it's as if someone's uncorked a bottle of laughter. We all break up. Nobody can stop.

"We . . . we just had to . . . to . . . drop in!" I gasp. "For a *flying* visit!"

"Just a *curtain* call," quips Harry emerging from a tangle of curtains. He drapes one across his nose like a veil.

Harry looks so funny we laugh even harder.

"But why so mysterious?" asks Pansy at last, taking off her pink glasses and wiping her eyes.

"Actually, we came to rescue Miss Tree . . ."

". . . from being drowned by dog dribble!" shouts Harry as Crusher slobbers over him. "Aaagh!"

When I've caught my breath I look up at Miss Tree. "We thought you'd been kidnapped. You disappeared so suddenly."

Miss Tree giggles. "Actually, I *was* hiding from my neighbours. I wanted to prepare *Peter Pan* in secret."

"I *knew* you were in here," I say, "when Barney sang his song. Well, Harry, the We-Solve-It Agency has solved its first big case."

Harry smiles. "Right. We solved the mystery of your disappearance," he says to Miss Tree. "But I'm just curious . . . why're you hanging from the ceiling?"

Miss Tree flaps her arms like wings. "Practising flying, of course. For *Peter Pan*."

Miss Tree calls down, "Everything is for the show. Costumes . . . scenery . . . Percy the parrot . . ."

"Percy the parrot. The Norwegian Blue." I smile. "Pansy, you sold him to *Miss Tree*."

Pansy nods. "Barney delivered him when he installed the flying equipment."

Barmy Barney. The Masked Man. "Would that be Barney from Maskerade?" I inquire, looking at my notes.

A small curly-haired man peeps out from the wings. "Barney, at your service," he sings.

I look at his grinning face. "Ever wear masks, Barney?"

Smiling, he sings: "There was a dance teacher named Tree . . ."

I laugh. Without a mask, he's just a nice little guy. I join in the song:

"Wanting *Peter Pan* stuff hurriedly . . ."

Harry joins in too. We all end up singing at the tops of our voices: "And flying equipment from me!"

"Barney's operating the flying equipment," says Miss Tree. "He installed it last night. Isn't it wonderful?"

"The banging!" Harry claps his hands to his head. "It was flying equipment being installed!"

"Ex . . . exactly."

"Ooohhh, Mari, what's the matter?" Harry says. "Your freckles have gone all blotchy . . ."

"Look . . ." I'm staring at the parrot's cage. "Look, Harry. I think we've found our pirate kidnapper as well . . ."

Harry laughs. "You're right! The shadow's like a pirate. Another mystery solved."

"You two always solve mysteries." Miss Tree does a little pirouette in the

air. "I might have known I couldn't hide from you."

I look up at her. "Well, we might have solved the mystery of your disappearance, but we have another problem to solve now."

"What's that?"

"How to convince your neighbours that Pear Tree School should stay open."

Miss Tree shouts down, "Surely when they hear Peter Pan's ear-piercing crow as he clashes swords with Captain Hook they'll be so impressed . . ."

"Er, I *don't* think so . . ." I interrupt. "Come on, think everybody. We *have* to think of something!"

Percy's idea is to drown the lot. Screeching about every man jack of 'em walking the plank, he knocks the mirror in his cage with his beak. Over and over. And as the mirror catches the lamplight outside, it hits me.

"The flashing signal! It was Percy's mirror!"

"Of course!"

We all burst into laughter again as Percy hits his mirror, over and over faster than a boxer with a punch-bag.

"Percy, you've been the culprit all along," says Harry wagging his finger at the bird. "First you squawk like a maniac so everyone thinks you're being kidnapped . . ."

"Then you signal with your mirror," says Pansy.

"But worst of all you disguise your cage as a pirate kidnapper," I laugh. "What's the matter with you? Do you want to play the part of Captain Hook?"

But I don't wait for a reply. Because a brilliant idea has just slipped into my head. It's so brilliant I should be moved to the top class overnight. I take a deep breath.

"Miss Tree, I have an idea. If we work together maybe we *can* change your neighbours' minds . . ."

Chapter Nine

The next day we call in the Prickly
Pear Street Gang to help.

We make posters and programmes;
paint scenery and sew costumes;
practise sword fights and flying . . .

Then we invite the neighbours over.
We show them the costumes.

Peter Pan
Costumes

We take them over the pirate ship.

We even let them try out the flying equipment.

They are most impressed.

But it's when they see our ideas for the cast, that they are completely won over.

PETER PAN

Produced and Directed
by Penelope Tree

STARRING:

Harry Hardcastle	as	Peter Pan
Marigold Masters	as	Captain Hook
Sadie Stretter	as	Wendy
Stretch	as	Michael
Squib	as	John
Mai Ling	as	Tiger Lily
Pete	as	An Indian Brave
The Pear Tree Gang	as	The Lost Boys

AND INTRODUCING:

Mr & Mrs Brown	as	Mr & Mrs Darling
Crusher	as	Nana
Pansy Potts	as	Tinker Bell
Barney	as	The Crocodile
Mr Parker	as	Smee
Percy Parrot	as	Percy Parrot

And so full rehearsals begin at last . . .
For the best production of *Peter Pan*
Prickly Pear City has ever seen.

Epilogue

You may be wondering why I went back to the pet shop.

Did I suspect the parrot buyer was Miss Tree?

Did I suspect Pansy was the kidnapper?

Well, yes and no.

Actually I went to buy a Pooper Scooper.

Mrs Brown loved it.

So did everyone on Prickly Pear Street.

Fighting crime. Keeping the streets clean.

It's my job.